GHASTLY BATTLE

GHASTLY BATTLE

AN UNOFFICIAL MINETRAPPED ADVENTURE, #4

Winter Morgan

Sky Pony Press
New York

Copyright © 2016 by Hollan Publishing, Inc.

Minecraft® is a registered trademark of Notch Development AB.

The Minecraft game is copyright © Mojang AB.

Sky Pony Press books may be purchased in bulk at special discounts for sales
promotion, corporate gifts, fund-raising, or educational purposes. Special
editions can also be created to specifications. For details, contact the Special
Sales Department, Sky Pony Press, 307 West 36th Street, 11th Floor,
New York, NY 10018 or info@skyhorsepublishing.com.

Sky Pony® is a registered trademark of Skyhorse Publishing, Inc.®,
a Delaware corporation.

Minecraft® is a registered trademark of Notch Development AB.
The Minecraft game is copyright © Mojang AB.

Visit our website at www.skyponypress.com.

10 9 8 7 6 5 4 3 2 1

Library of Congress Cataloging-in-Publication Data is available on file.

Cover design by Brian Peterson
Cover photo by Megan Miller

Print ISBN: 978-1-5107-0600-2
Ebook ISBN: 978-1-5107-0610-1

Printed in Canada

TABLE OF CONTENTS

GHASTLY BATTLE

1

NEW ARRIVALS

Simon kept a close eye on his inventory. "We have to make sure there is enough wood."

"We'll be fine. If we run out of supplies, we'll just stop and get more," Michael dismissed Simon's comment.

"I don't like to start a project I can't finish." Simon was annoyed.

"We can finish it, but we might have to pause in the middle to get some more wood," Michael clarified.

Lily walked over. "What are you building?"

"We're building a carousel. I was thinking we could use some redstone," said Simon.

"That sounds like fun," replied Lily as she eyed their large roller coaster. She had built that coaster with Michael and Simon, and now they were building a carousel on their own. "You're building it right by the roller coaster?"

"Yes," explained Michael. "We want to make an amusement park."

Lily felt a lump in her throat. "It seems like a rather large project for two people."

"Do you think we need help?" asked Simon.

Lily tried to hide her disappointment. "I guess you can do it on your own."

"Is everything okay, Lily?" Michael put down his supplies and walked over to his friend.

"Yes." Lily wiped the tears from her eyes.

Simon rushed over. "What is it?"

"I feel left out. We always built everything together, and now you're doing this on your own. Why didn't you think to invite me?" She frowned.

"We just forgot. We didn't mean to upset you," Simon stammered.

"You forgot about me?" Lily was hurt.

"We always like building with you," Michael explained.

"Yes," Simon added. "We just walked over here and had the idea to build a carousel. Of course we were going to ask you."

Matthew thought for a moment. "I guess we've all gotten used to being a bit more independent since being trapped on the server. But we have to remember how important our friendships are and work together as a team. Lily, would you please help us build this carousel?"

Lily smiled. "Thanks. I'd love to help you guys."

"Do you have any redstone?" Simon asked as he perused his inventory for the second time.

Lily studied her inventory and suggested, "An amusement park is a big project. Why don't we invite other people from the town to help? I'm sure Warren, Robin, Ilana, Peter, George, and Sarah would want to build an amusement park with us. And I bet there would be even more people excited about it, too."

"Yes, we should make this a team effort," Simon agreed.

"That's a fantastic idea," Michael exclaimed.

"Come with me," Lily said. "Let's ask the towns-people to help us." Her two friends followed her back into the center of Lisimi Village.

"I hope we find someone to help quickly. I really want to get back to work," Michael remarked.

As they reached the center of the town, Lily thought about a name for the amusement park. "Should we name it Lisimi Land?"

"Or we can name it Adventure Park and make a bunch of adventure courses," suggested Simon.

"What about Fun Park?" Michael added.

As the trio bounced around various names for their amusement park, they stumbled upon two people who looked lost. The strangers stood by a tree, looking off in the direction of the town.

"Can you help us?" the girl, who was wearing a pink beret, called out. She was shaking and seemed very upset. "We see there is a town in the distance."

"I see an iron golem," said the boy, who was wear-ing a black suit.

"We're lost," admitted the girl.

"Are you okay?" Lily asked.

The girl in the pink beret shook as she spoke. "No. I think something has gone very wrong."

"Yes, incredibly wrong," added her friend. His voice cracked. "I think we are actually *in* a Minecraft game. We were playing, and we got zapped into this game."

Lily's heart started to beat rapidly. She couldn't believe more people had been zapped onto the server when all of the griefers responsible for sucking people into the game had been imprisoned. Seeing these two new people not only shocked her, it also scared her; she wondered who had trapped them on the server.

"Can you tell us your story?" Michael asked. "How were you zapped onto the server?"

Lily nodded encouragingly. "I know you're upset, but please, tell us what you can remember. We want to help you and this is an important step in figuring out how you were trapped on the server."

The girl wearing the pink beret introduced herself first. "I'm Blossom. I was playing on a server with my friends and then it just shut off."

"It's not that simple," the boy in the black suit added. "We were in the middle of unearthing treasure. It was so annoying because we lost the treasure, and now we're actually in Minecraft. I didn't even know that was possible."

Blossom explained how they were both playing Minecraft at her house when it happened. "The game shut off as we were unearthing the treasure and when we turned our computers back on, the lights shut off in my house and we were zapped onto the server."

"That's awful," Lily exclaimed. "We know how hard it is to adjust, but we'll help you," she reassured them.

"But we have to find out who zapped them onto this server," Michael added.

"Yes, we do." Lily wondered if there was another griefer in the Overworld who had the power to zap people onto the server. Lily was terrified that there was an unknown, powerful griefer in the Overworld.

Michael uttered, "This isn't going to be easy."

Lily gave him a dirty look. She didn't want to frighten the newcomers.

Simon looked up at the sky. "It's almost night, and we have to get back to the village."

"Do you have a place where we can stay?" asked Blossom. "I can't bear to battle any hostile mobs in real life."

"Yes." Michael offered them a room in his house.

"Thanks," said the boy in the black suit, and then he finally introduced himself. "I'm Sunny. I forgot to mention that when we were unearthing the treasure, we saw other treasure hunters, and they started to attack us."

"Do you think they had something to do with trapping you on the server?" asked Michael.

"I'm not sure," replied Sunny.

"What did they look like?" asked Simon.

"I didn't see them for very long, but they were wearing blue hats, which I thought was very strange," said Sunny.

"Blue hats. I don't know anyone who wears a blue hat." Lily tried to figure out who wanted Blossom and Sunny's treasure.

"Did you hear them call out any names?" questioned Michael.

Blossom stammered, "Um, no. It all happened so quickly. I wasn't paying attention, I just wanted to get the treasure and TP back to our village. And then the lights went out and we were trapped on this server."

"This is so similar to how we were trapped. Our parents were calling to us to stop playing because there was a powerful storm in our town, but we were trying to stop a gang of griefers from attacking our roller coaster. If only we had shut the computer down and stopped playing, we wouldn't be trapped on this server, too." Simon's eyes filled with tears.

"I'm sorry. I didn't mean to upset you." Blossom looked at Simon.

Lily didn't want to focus on the negative or the reason they were trapped on the server. She wanted to get to the bottom of this mystery. "We will find out who trapped you on this server," she declared.

"And you'll definitely get us home?" asked Blossom.

Lily opened her mouth to answer, but she didn't know how to respond.

2

ESCAPE

Lily couldn't even figure out how to get *herself* off the server, so she wasn't sure how she'd get Blossom and Sunny back home. She had seen others, like the Prismarines and Georgia, get zapped back to the real world, but it had been a while since anyone had made their way back home, and she was getting discouraged. Lily might have hoped that meeting Blossom and Sunny would energize her and inspire her to think of new ways to escape, but instead it just made her feel helpless.

"I will try my hardest," Lily promised Blossom and Sunny, nonetheless.

"We have to pick up the speed," Simon reminded them. "It's getting dark, and soon hostile mobs will spawn."

"Too late," Michael cried. "Skeletons!"

Arrows flew through the sky, and as one punctured Blossom's arm, she wailed, "It hurts a lot more in real life!"

"It's going to be okay," Lily reassured her as she leapt toward the bony mob with her diamond sword.

As Blossom watched Lily, she bit her lip, then tossed her fears aside and lunged at a skeleton, destroying the creature with three strikes from her diamond sword. She called out to Sunny, "It's not as bad as you think. Just start fighting."

Sunny reluctantly grabbed his sword and struck a skeleton that was trying to attack him.

The skeleton fighting Blossom shot another arrow at her, piercing her other arm. "Ouch!" Blossom screamed, as she leapt toward the skeleton and delivered a final blow, destroying the beast.

Blossom picked up the bone the skeleton had dropped on the ground when it was destroyed. She began to feel more confident, and she smiled as she struck another skeleton that charged toward the group.

"Good job!" Lily called out. "You're getting the hang of this rather quickly."

With another couple of strikes from her sword, Blossom was able to obliterate another block-headed skeleton. Then she turned around and, to her horror and surprise, saw a band of zombies marching toward them.

Lily sprinted toward the zombies and splashed potions on them. As she ran, she called to the others, "We have to stay near the iron golem, where zombies can't spawn."

The others agreed as they annihilated the vacant-eyed, undead mobs that strutted toward them. When the final zombie was destroyed, Michael said, "We need to get to safety. My house is the closest. We should all go there and hide."

"Sounds like a plan." Lily could barely get the words out as she ran as fast as she could toward Michael's house. When they opened the door, they each hurried to a bed and dove beneath the covers.

As Blossom pulled the covers over herself, she said, "Thanks for letting us stay here. This has been quite an awful adventure so far. I just want to go home."

Sunny sniffled as tears streamed down his cheeks. "I miss my bed."

"Me too," Blossom sobbed.

"Why would someone do this to us?" Sunny asked.

Simon explained, "We know why the person who trapped us on this server zapped us here. He's a master griefer named Mr. Anarchy. We have no idea who zapped you onto this server, but I assume they did it for the same reason. They were upset that they are trapped here and wanted to zap more people in."

Lily added, "We've been stuck here for a long time, and we never thought about trapping other people on the server. We just focus on trying to get out."

Simon agreed, "We're also trying to have fun while we're here. We love Minecraft, and it's fun to do cool things like build rides for our amusement park."

"You're building an amusement park?" Blossom perked up.

Michael described the amusement park, and soon everyone drifted off to sleep, lulled by the sound of his voice, and dreamed about the park and the different rides they were going to create.

Blossom was the first to wake. She rushed to the window, catching a glimpse of the sunrise over Lisimi Village.

"It's so pretty," Blossom exclaimed.

The rest of the gang got up, and Lily offered everyone cake. Blossom took a bite. "This tastes so much different than I imagined."

"Everything is different," Michael reminded her.

"At least there aren't any hostile mobs spawning during the day," Sunny said as he took a large bite from the cake.

"Yes, this means we can spend the day working on the amusement park. We still don't have a name for it. What did you want to call it again, Lily?" asked Michael. "Lisimi Land?"

"The amusement park?" Blossom asked. "I think we should spend the day working on ways to get off the server." Blossom was angry. She wanted her new friends to help her get back home.

"We are always plotting new ways to get home, but we're also going to build a super awesome amusement park," Simon didn't want to fight with these new players. He knew how hard it was to adjust to living in the game, but he also wanted to focus on his new project.

Blossom suggested, "We will help you with amusement park if you can tell us how others have left the server."

"Deal," Simon said.

The gang was ready to leave to work on the amusement park when Robin and Peter ran into Michael's house.

Robin cried, "I have bad news."

"What?" Lily was worried.

"It's Mr. Anarchy." Peter's voice shook.

"What about him?" Michael demanded.

"Isn't Mr. Anarchy the person who trapped you on this server?" questioned Blossom.

"Yes," Robin answered, "and he's escaped!"

3
NEW VILLAINS

"**N**ow we know who trapped Blossom and Sunny on this server," Lily said.

"We can't be certain of that," Michael said. "When did Mr. Anarchy escape?"

"Just now," said Peter.

"Two people wearing blue hats sprinted into town, shooting arrows at everyone," Robin told them. "They destroyed the guards at the prison and set Mr. Anarchy free."

"Blue hats!" Blossom gasped.

"The griefers!" Sunny exclaimed.

"What about Matthew, Otto, and Emma? Did they escape?" Simon questioned.

"I think they're still there. I didn't see them escape with Mr. Anarchy," Peter spoke quickly.

"We need to see them," Michael said, and he dashed to the prison. The others followed.

"Michael's right," Simon confirmed. "I bet Matthew, Otto, and Emma know who is behind this escape."

The group hurried over to the prison. When they approached the jail, they saw the prison guards respawn.

One of the prison guards apologized for letting Mr. Anarchy escape. "It happened so quickly. I didn't have any time to react."

"It's not your fault," Lily told them.

Robin said, "I was in the village when the two people in blue hats came running into town, and they were very powerful. It was a surprise attack, and you did the best job you could."

"Thanks," the guard replied.

Michael questioned, "Was there anything that stood out about the attacks? Did you recognize the people who took Mr. Anarchy? Was Mr. Anarchy acting strangely over the last few days?"

The guards were overwhelmed by the numerous questions. One of the guards spoke slowly, trying to remember every detail of the escape. "I can't say that Mr. Anarchy was acting any differently than he usually acts. We weren't expecting this attack, and the people came in very quickly. We had no time to react."

When it was clear they weren't going to get any more information from the guards, the gang visited Emma, Otto, and Matthew. But all three of them claimed they knew nothing about Mr. Anarchy's plan to escape.

Emma remarked, "If we did know, don't you think we would have gone with him?"

Lily inspected Mr. Anarchy's small prison cell to see if there were any clues. A lone silverfish crawled across the floor in the dimly lit room. She plunged her sword into the monster, destroying it with one strike from her sword. But as her sword hit the ground, the block it struck broke.

"I thought this was a bedrock room. How can a block in its floor break?" Lily questioned.

The group was stunned. But before anyone had a chance to respond, thunder boomed throughout the town.

"Someone summoned a storm!" Simon hollered.

"Are you sure it's not a natural storm?" asked Sunny.

"No, we've seen this before." Michael stared at Emma, Otto, and Matthew as he spoke.

Matthew shrugged. "We didn't have anything to do with this storm, I promise. We've been trapped in this prison."

Michael was too busy battling the zombies that lumbered toward the prison to respond.

Ilana sprinted into the village, armed with a bunch of potions. She splashed potions on the zombies, weakening them. Lily and Robin plunged their swords into the weakened zombies, effortlessly destroying each one.

But no matter how many zombies they destroyed, more crept toward the town. The iron golem did little to stop the zombie invasion.

"We need to end this storm and find the monster spawner that's creating all of these zombies." Michael was annoyed. He wanted to find Mr. Anarchy, and this zombie attack was wasting his time.

"I bet the griefers in the blue hats staged this attack so they had time to escape," Lily said as she exhaustedly destroyed another zombie.

Without warning, the sun came out, and the zombies disappeared. "Finally," uttered Michael.

Lily and the others ran back to the prison. They rushed into Emma, Otto, and Matthew's cell and interrogated them.

Simon asked, "What do you know?"

Robin demanded, "Tell us, now!"

"We are innocent," Emma pleaded. "Leave us alone."

"We don't believe you." Michael was frustrated.

"We don't have any information!" Otto screamed. "Leave, now!"

Lily was frustrated. She wasn't getting any information from Emma, Otto, and Matthew, and she was beginning to lose hope. "This is pointless."

Peter reassured her, "We will get answers. We can't give up."

Everyone turned around when Juan ran into the prison.

Juan breathlessly exclaimed, "I have very important news."

"What?" Lily asked.

"I've seen the two people who helped Mr. Anarchy escape. They came into my butcher shop yesterday," said Juan.

Everyone's eyes widened at the news. Lily remarked, "They must have been staying close to the town."

Robin asked, "Did they talk to you?"

"Yes," Juan recalled, "they spoke to me. They wore blue hats, so I know they were the same people. They asked me lots of questions about griefers and all of the trouble we've had in Lisimi Village, and about the prison."

"Did you answer them?" asked Lily.

"I told them we had the griefer situation under control and that the villains were in prison. I feel awful, like I gave them too much info," confessed Juan.

"You didn't do anything wrong," Lily reassured him.

A voice boomed, "She's right. You didn't do anything wrong, Juan."

The gang swiftly turned around and saw Mr. Anarchy standing in the center of the village. He held a diamond sword and stood next to the two people who had rescued him from the prison.

"What do you want from us, Mr. Anarchy?" Lily shouted.

"Haven't you done enough damage?" Michael hollered.

"No," he smiled. "I guess I haven't. You can't stop me. Can't you see how I was able to trap people on the server when I was in prison? There's no way you can control my actions. I'm too powerful."

Lily called out, "Are you done gloating yet?"

Blossom shook as she stood face-to-face with the person who admitted to trapping her on the server. She wanted to destroy him. She shouted, "Why us? Why did you trap us on the server?"

Sunny screamed, "I want to go home."

"We all do, right?" Mr. Anarchy looked over at his sinister sidekicks, but they didn't acknowledge Mr. Anarchy's question. He repeated it, "Don't we all want to leave this server?"

The two ignored him and crafted a portal to the Nether. Mr. Anarchy didn't help them. He stood silently by, looking confused. Sweat formed above his brow as he watched Lily trying to stop the two people who he had thought were his sidekicks. When they had offered to help him escape the prison, Mr. Anarchy had assumed they wanted to help him escape, and thought he could help them, in turn. But now Mr. Anarchy wondered if Pablo and Ronan were really running the show, and if he was their sidekick.

Mr. Anarchy gasped as Lily shot an arrow at Pablo and Ronan, but they dodged it and continued to construct the portal.

Blossom was infuriated. Mr. Anarchy wasn't paying attention and didn't notice Blossom as she sprinted toward him. She made the most of the opportunity and struck the evil griefer with her sword.

Taken by surprise, Mr. Anarchy didn't have time to grab his sword and fight back. To escape, he hopped on the portal to the Nether, while Pablo and Ronan ignited it. As purple mist surrounded them, Blossom jumped onto the portal with Mr. Anarchy, and the whole group disappeared into the Nether.

4
ESCAPE TO THE NETHER

"**B**lossom!" Sunny shouted to his friend as she disappeared into the fiery biome.

"We need to find her," Lily said, grabbing obsidian from her inventory. "I only have a couple of blocks. Does anybody have obsidian?"

"Yes," Peter said, and he placed two blocks of obsidian, completing the rectangle. "We just have to ignite it."

Sunny was the first to hop on the portal. "We need to find Blossom."

"And stop Mr. Anarchy," Michael reminded them.

"I'm not worried about Mr. Anarchy. I just want to find Blossom," Sunny reiterated.

"We know you do, but if we don't find Mr. Anarchy, more people will be zapped onto this server," Peter called out as the purple mist surrounded them and they arrived in the fiery Nether landscape.

Sunny gasped. "This isn't what I expected."

"Watch out!" Lily cried. "Ghasts!"

Michael's eyes widened as he watched an endless number of ghasts flying through the air. "I've never seen this many ghasts in my life."

"This is highly unusual. Someone must be behind this attack," Lily theorized.

"I agree," Simon said as he grabbed his bow and arrow and aimed at the flying white beasts. "It has to be Mr. Anarchy and his evil minions."

"I miss Blossom!" Sunny called out.

"This isn't the time to look for your friend. We have to fight to survive." Michael looked over at Sunny. "Use your fists to deflect the fireballs."

"I have snowballs." Sunny took a couple of snowballs from his inventory and threw them at the ghasts, destroying two of them.

"Excellent!" Michael smiled.

Lily struck a fireball with her fist and it flew toward the ghast that had shot it, destroying the blocky white mob.

Several of the ghasts unleashed high-pitched sounds that deafened the gang. Sunny cried out, "Make them stop!"

"We can't!" Lily used her fists to destroy as many ghasts as she could. "The only way of stopping them is destroying them."

Robin aimed her bow and arrow at the ghasts, striking a few. Michael threw his last remaining snowballs at the floating mobs. Lily used her fists, since her inventory was dangerously low. As Peter aimed his arrow at a ghast, Lily cried out, "Watch out! You're on the edge of a lava river."

Peter looked down. "Thank you! I was so distracted by the battle, I didn't notice the lava."

"The Nether is awful," Sunny declared as she threw his final snowball at a ghast and destroyed it.

Lily tried to be optimistic. "I think we've destroyed a bunch of the ghasts. We're going to be okay."

"You spoke too soon," Michael hollered as a gang of blazes flew beside the ghasts.

"Blazes!" Sunny was terrified. He was scared of blazes when he played the game, and now he had to encounter them in real life. He began to shake. "What am I supposed to do? I am out of snowballs."

Ilana exclaimed, "I don't have any fire resistance potions."

Peter called out, "I have some snowballs, Sunny."

Sunny and Peter concentrated as they threw the snowballs. They didn't have that many, and they had to use them wisely to destroy the blazes.

Lily and Robin annihilated the last few ghasts and helped the others defeat the blazes. When every flying, hostile Nether mob was destroyed, Sunny asked, "Can we look for Blossom now? I am very worried about her."

"We understand," Lily reassured him. "We will help your friend."

Peter broke away from the group and walked along the lava river, calling out to the others, "I see a Nether fortress."

"Where?" Ilana raced to Peter's side.

"It's behind that large pillar." He pointed out the Nether fortress in the distance.

"That's so far off," Sunny cried.

"I know, but it might contain treasure," Peter reminded him.

"And a bunch of fantastic resources for brewing potions like netherrack, which I desperately need," added Ilana.

"Also, that's the type of place where Mr. Anarchy and his minions might be hiding," Michael suggested.

"Do you think Blossom is in the Nether fortress?" Sunny was extremely hopeful.

"We won't know until we travel there," Lily said, and the gang walked along the lava river toward the large fortress.

As they neared the structure, three blazes shot fire-balls at them. As the group battled the pesky mobs, they heard the roar of a familiar voice coming from inside the Nether fortress.

5

OVERHEARD

Mr. Anarchy howled, "Pablo and Ronan, you aren't what I thought you were! You said you were here to help."

"Shh!" Lily told the others. She peeked her head inside the Nether fortress. "We can't let him know we're here."

Ilana whispered, "Maybe we should use a potion of invisibility?"

"Good idea," Lily said, and Ilana handed the potion out to the others.

One by one, the group sipped the potion and began to disappear. They walked into the Nether fortress just as the argument escalated between Mr. Anarchy and the griefers.

"How could you do this to me?" Mr. Anarchy cried.

"You're done," Ronan yelled. "Your game is over. We control this server now. You didn't follow our rules, so now you have to pay the price."

"But to actually use command blocks to put me on Hardcore mode and destroy me? That's horrible. I won't only be erased from the game, I might possibly be erased from existence!" Mr. Anarchy cried.

"That's a chance we're willing to take," Pablo said as he placed command blocks in the corner of the Nether fortress and began to place Mr. Anarchy on Hardcore mode.

"You were never really that evil," remarked Ronan.

"What?" Mr. Anarchy was confused.

"And you weren't that smart either. You got caught. We had to help you escape from prison. If you were a true evil mastermind, you wouldn't have been rotting away in a bedrock prison!" shouted Pablo.

"But it wasn't really about being evil. I wanted to escape. I wanted—I still want—to go home. I have been stuck on this server for such a long time. It's hard to be here. You know how I feel; both of you wanted to get zapped back to the real world," Mr. Anarchy sobbed.

"And you did a great job getting us back home, didn't you?" Ronan stood by the command blocks and yelled at Mr. Anarchy.

"You promised to get us back home, and you failed. Now you're going to be punished." Pablo walked over to the command blocks.

"Please," Mr. Anarchy pleaded, "don't destroy me."

"You destroyed yourself." Ronan walked toward Mr. Anarchy and held his sword against his chest.

"I tried," Mr. Anarchy confessed. "I really tried to send you home. But I don't know how to get off this server. If I did, would I still be here?"

"So you admit you're a liar?" Ronan's blade rubbed against Mr. Anarchy's arm.

"I wouldn't say a liar. I mean, I'm trying to figure out how to get off the server, and I did get others off," Mr. Anarchy explained.

"But you just said you didn't know how to escape." Ronan raised his voice.

"We've had enough of you, Mr. Anarchy!" Pablo screamed as he worked on the command blocks.

"But I can help you," Mr. Anarchy whimpered.

"How?" Pablo looked up.

"I'm the only one who can zap people onto this server. Haven't I done enough? You made me prove my power by zapping those two people onto the server the other day. You know I didn't want to do it, but I did it for you," Mr. Anarchy spoke hurriedly, trying to prove his worth.

Sunny's heart was beating rapidly, but he couldn't do anything about how upset he was. He was so angry that he and Blossom were randomly zapped onto the server to prove Mr. Anarchy's strength and power that he wanted to attack Mr. Anarchy and the two griefers, but he knew he couldn't let them know the gang was there. He had to stick with his friends and stay invisible, but this seemed like an impossible challenge.

Pablo said, "So you can zap people onto the server. Is that your only trick?"

"No! I did get that girl Blossom back home," Mr. Anarchy said.

"That was an accident," Ronan said. "You didn't know how that happened. When we arrived here, she was gone."

Pablo added, "We don't know for sure that she got back home. It could have been a glitch. Maybe she respawned somewhere else in the Nether."

"Okay. Forget about Blossom. I can't take credit for that," admitted Mr. Anarchy.

"I guess you don't have as many skills as you think," Ronan said.

"I'm also a master at creating storms and destroying Lisimi Village. I know these people, and I know their weaknesses." Mr. Anarchy smiled. "That must make me worth something, right?"

Pablo and Ronan paused. They walked to the corner of the fortress to discuss this alone. Pablo looked over at Mr. Anarchy. "Don't go anywhere. or I will put you on Hardcore mode. You are so weak, it would take one blast from a ghast to destroy you."

"Why would I leave?" asked Mr. Anarchy. "I want to work with you."

As Ronan and Pablo talked, a bouncing noise emanated from another room.

"What's that?" cried Ronan.

Mr. Anarchy said, "It sounds like magma cubes. Have you ever fought these in the real world?"

"Yes," Pablo declared, grabbing his sword from his inventory and lunging at the three cubes that bounced into the center of the room.

Ronan struck one of the cubes and it broke into smaller cubes. He tried to obliterate the smaller cubes, but he was having a tough time. "Aren't you going to help us?" he called out to Mr. Anarchy.

"Now you need my help?" Mr. Anarchy said.

"Yes," Pablo shouted, "now!"

"But I am very low on energy," Mr. Anarchy reminded them.

Pablo took milk from his inventory and handed it to Mr. Anarchy. "Drink this, then help us defeat these magma cubes."

Ronan annihilated two cubes, but three more bounced down the hall.

Mr. Anarchy slayed a cube with his diamond sword and gasped when he saw a blaze fly through the Nether fortress.

Ronan tried to dodge the blast, but it didn't work. He was struck by the fireball and lost a heart.

Pablo was also struck by the fireball's blast, and he cried out.

Mr. Anarchy destroyed the ghast and the final magma cubes. "See? I am worth something," Mr. Anarchy declared.

Ronan and Pablo weren't listening. They were too busy staring at the players that stood in the center of the Nether fortress.

Lily looked at her hands and panicked. They weren't invisible.

6

FAMILIAR FACE

"Lily!" Mr. Anarchy said. "And your friends. What a pleasant surprise."

Pablo looked at Mr. Anarchy. "How did they find us?"

Sunny cried out, "Where's Blossom?"

"Blossom is back in the real world," Ronan said. "Or, at least, we think she is."

"I want to find her." Sunny was frustrated.

"If you can get back to the real world, please let us know how." Ronan clutched his diamond sword and walked toward Sunny.

"We aren't here to fight you," Lily announced.

"Really? Then why are you here?" questioned Pablo.

"We want to bring Mr. Anarchy back to the prison. He caused a lot of trouble and he deserves to be there," explained Michael.

"You can have him," Pablo laughed. "He's useless to us."

"What?" Mr. Anarchy cried, but he stopped when he stared at the command blocks. He knew Pablo and Ronan hadn't activated them yet, and he wanted to destroy them before they could put him on Hardcore mode.

"Now that you have Mr. Anarchy, can you leave us alone?" Ronan demanded.

Lily looked over at her friends. She knew they had to attack Ronan and Pablo, because they were griefers. If the gang let this duo escape, they could unleash a horrible attack on the Overworld, and they had the potential to destroy Lisimi Village. Yet Lily didn't know how to communicate with her friends as they stood face-to-face with these griefers. Instead of talking, she grabbed a potion of harming and splashed it on Pablo and Ronan.

"No!" screamed a weakened Pablo.

Lily charged toward Pablo and Ronan with her diamond sword, striking both of them.

Mr. Anarchy stood in the corner, destroying the command blocks. When he was finished, he sprinted toward Lily and joined her in battling the two griefers.

"What are you doing?" Lily was shocked.

"I'm on your side now. These guys made me do things I never wanted to do. I didn't want to zap Blossom and Sunny on the server," Mr. Anarchy told the gang.

"He's a liar!" Ronan could barely spit out these words. He was losing energy. He tried to get milk or a potion of healing from his inventory, but he was too weak.

Michael slammed his sword against Pablo and destroyed him.

"My friend!" Ronan cried out to Pablo as he was destroyed.

"You're next," Simon stood next to weakened Ronan.

Ronan looked over at Mr. Anarchy. "Help me!" he pleaded.

"Never." Mr. Anarchy delivered the final blow that destroyed Ronan.

Lily looked at Mr. Anarchy. "This doesn't mean you're off the hook."

Robin, Ilana, Peter, Sunny, Michael, Simon, and Lily crowded around Mr. Anarchy.

Robin said, "We were here the entire time. We heard you talking to Pablo and Ronan. We know you tried to sell yourself as a great griefer."

"Yes, we heard you talk about attacking Lisimi Village," Ilana added.

"But I was just trying to save myself. They were putting me on Hardcore mode. You saw the command blocks," Mr. Anarchy defended himself.

"We can't trust you," Lily told him.

"I can help you defeat Pablo and Ronan. They have an awful plan for Lisimi Village and I can help you stop it," confessed Mr. Anarchy.

"Why should we believe you?" Simon held his sword against Mr. Anarchy's chest.

"Why would I lie? I am going back to the village. If we're under attack, I will be helpless in the prison," explained Mr. Anarchy.

Lily paused. She didn't know if they should work with Mr. Anarchy. She wanted to have a meeting with her friends, but they didn't have any time, because six ghasts shot through the Nether fortress and the group was suddenly surrounded by a sea of fireballs.

Lily used her remaining couple of arrows to destroy a ghast. The gang pooled together whatever snowballs they had to battle the fiery mobs. Mr. Anarchy had good aim and obliterated two ghasts with snowballs of his own.

Lily looked over at Mr. Anarchy fighting alongside them. She was conflicted. As a group of magma cubes bounced toward them, she could hear cries coming from down the hall. Lily was too busy battling the cubes while dodging the blasts from the ghasts to find out who was whimpering down the hall.

The gang used all of their resources in battle. Simon slammed his diamond sword into several magma cubes, destroying both the larger cubes and the smaller ones.

When the final cube was annihilated, Lily left her friends and stalked down the hall toward the sound of the cries. As she reached the lava room, the cries grew louder. Lily walked into the room and spotted Blossom standing in the corner, weeping.

"Lily! You're alive!" Blossom called out.

"What are you doing here? We thought you made it back to the real world." Lily was shocked to see Blossom.

"Ronan told me everyone was put on Hardcore mode and destroyed." Blossom wiped the tears from her eyes.

"How did you get here?" Lily asked.

"When we emerged in the Nether, I was alone. I spotted Ronan and tried to run from him, but he was too fast and caught up to me," Blossom blurted out. "He marched me into this fortress and told me to stay here until he called for me. He said he put Mr. Anarchy and everyone else on Hardcore mode and they were all destroyed. He claimed if I waited here, I'd be safe. I didn't know what to do," Blossom sobbed.

"It's going to be okay." Lily tried to comfort her new friend, but she wasn't sure she was telling the truth.

7
POOLS OF LAVA

michael rushed down the hall and called to the others, "Lily found Blossom."

"That's impossible," Sunny cried. "She's back home, in the real world."

"No, I'm not," Blossom replied. "I was trapped by Ronan."

"But Ronan and Pablo said you vanished." Mr. Anarchy was confused.

"They lied," Lily stared at Mr. Anarchy. "Which is why I will never trust a griefer."

"You can trust me," Mr. Anarchy told them.

"You're joking." Michael chuckled.

Mr. Anarchy was irritated. "If I was really working with Pablo and Ronan, I'd know that they had trapped Blossom, right?"

Lily understood Mr. Anarchy's logic, but she still didn't trust him. "You zapped us on this server and ruined our lives. When we arrived here, you imprisoned us and attacked our peaceful village, and now that you've been abandoned by your griefer friends, you think we will instantly forgive you?"

"Um," Mr. Anarchy stammered. "I guess—"

But Mr. Anarchy couldn't finish his sentence, because there was a loud roar from outside the Nether fortress.

"It's the Ender Dragon!" Ilana screamed.

"I bet Ronan and Pablo are back in the Nether. They probably summoned it," Michael called out as he ran out of the Nether fortress, clutching his bow and arrow.

The gang followed Michael out of the Nether fortress. Ilana passed a patch of netherrack and was upset that she didn't have any time to pick it. This was a vital ingredient for her potions, and she was running low on all of her potions. But she gathered the strength to pass up the valuable resource and sprinted toward the sound of the Ender Dragon instead.

The muscular beast's wing slammed into the Nether fortress, and the gang shielded themselves from the rubble.

Simon and Lily shot arrows that pierced the side of the dragon, and it roared in pain.

"The dragon is losing hearts," Robin pointed out as she struck the dragon with her diamond sword.

The powerful beast lunged at Robin, crushing her with its powerful tail. Robin had one heart left, and used her last bit of energy to strike the dragon, but it was pointless. The dragon roared and struck Robin with its scaly wing, destroying her.

"Robin!" Lily cried out.

"It's okay. She'll respawn in Lisimi Village," Simon reassured his friend.

Lily was infuriated, and she grabbed her sword and pounded it into the flying menace. The dragon tried to wipe Lily out with its tail, but she was a skilled fighter and redoubled her attacks, annihilating the dragon. It dropped an egg, and a portal to the End spawned in front of Lily.

"Good job," a voice called out.

Lily looked up and saw Ronan and Pablo standing in front of her.

"I don't need any compliments from you." She glared at the two griefers.

Pablo looked over at Blossom. "How did you respawn? I thought you were in the real world."

"Ask your friend Ronan," Blossom replied.

"What are you talking about?" Pablo was confused.

Ronan fumbled with words. "At first I thought she was missing, but then I found her in the Nether, and I didn't know what to do."

"That's right, I was never in the real world. Your friend tricked you," declared Blossom.

"I didn't trick you. I was going to tell you," Ronan explained.

Pablo grabbed his sword and held it against Ronan's chest, but he noticed everyone staring at them. He knew that he must forgive Ronan in order to maintain their power and control. Pablo put the sword back in his inventory and said, "I believe you."

Lily didn't want to stand around and watch two evil griefers bicker. "I guess you can sort out your problems when we bring you back to Lisimi Village and place you in the bedrock prison," she said.

Pablo took a potion of harming from his inventory and yelled, "We will never be one of your prisoners." He splashed the potion on the gang.

Lily was weak, but she was still able to grab some milk from her inventory, and she took a sip, then passed the milk to her friends.

With renewed energy, Lily lunged at Pablo and struck him with her diamond sword.

Ronan tried to help his friend, but he was distracted when four ghasts shot through the sky. Two of the ghasts shot fireballs in Ronan's direction. He tried to deflect the first fireball with his fist, but he couldn't. Ronan was destroyed.

"Ronan!" Pablo called out.

Lily didn't want to destroy Pablo; she wanted to capture him and place him in the bedrock prison. When Michael struck Pablo with his diamond sword, she told him to stop.

Lily stared into Pablo's eyes. "You're coming back to Lisimi Village with us."

"Never!" He could barely spit the word out as he turned away from Lily. Rather than be captured, Pablo walked right toward the ghast's fireball and was destroyed.

The whole gang gasped, but they couldn't spend long thinking about Pablo and Ronan—the ghasts were still attacking.

"Where are they respawning?" Lily questioned Mr. Anarchy.

"I don't know," Mr. Anarchy said as he destroyed a ghast with an arrow.

"We don't have any more snowballs left," Sunny announced as he destroyed another ghast with an arrow.

"There's only one ghast left," Simon remarked. "We can destroy it."

Ilana punched a fireball and redirected it to destroy the final ghast.

"We have to get back to Lisimi Village," Lily suggested.

Before anyone had a chance to respond, Ronan and Pablo appeared in front of them.

"You're back," Lily screamed. "Now we will take you prisoner."

"Funny, we came back to destroy you," Ronan snickered.

"You'll never succeed," declared Peter.

"Maybe, but we're going to try." Pablo smiled.

Ronan walked over to Mr. Anarchy. "We've also come back for you."

Mr. Anarchy was stunned. "You want me back?"

8

FIRE RESISTANT

Lily stared at Mr. Anarchy. She wanted him to make the right decision, and she wanted to believe that he had changed.

Mr. Anarchy looked at Pablo and Ronan. "But why? You said you didn't need me anymore."

"We were wrong," Pablo admitted.

"We need you," Ronan confessed.

Mr. Anarchy stood silently. He also feared that they might have him on Hardcore mode, and if he stayed with Lily and her friends, he might be destroyed. He looked at the gang from Lisimi Village. They had so much to offer him and were the nicest people he'd ever met. He felt this overwhelming guilt for trapping them on the server and wanted to redeem himself by helping them escape the server.

Lily didn't give Mr. Anarchy a chance to choose between the paths of good and evil. She quickly leapt at Ronan, striking him with great force.

The gang joined her in battling the two griefers. Mr. Anarchy just stood and watched. When Ronan and Pablo each had one heart left, Lily rushed over to Mr. Anarchy. "Make a portal to the Overworld," she said.

"I can't," he whispered to Lily. "I'm sorry. They might have me on Hardcore mode, and if they destroy me, I'll be gone forever. I have to go."

"Mr. Anarchy!" Lily cried as Mr. Anarchy splashed a potion on himself and disappeared.

Ilana called out, "Mr. Anarchy is gone!"

"Where did he go?" Peter asked.

"Did anyone see him use a potion of invisibility?" asked Ilana.

"I wasn't watching him," said Michael, and the others said the same. Everyone was busy battling Ronan and Pablo to pay attention to Mr. Anarchy.

Lily didn't say anything about what she'd seen. She didn't want to focus on Mr. Anarchy's disappearance, because she understood why he left. She wanted to get the two griefers into the bedrock prison in Lisimi Village. "I'm out of obsidian," she said, changing the subject. "Does anyone have some?"

Peter and Michael grabbed obsidian from their inventories and crafted a portal.

Ronan and Pablo reluctantly stepped aboard, but before the gang ignited the portal they heard Sunny scream, "Oh no!"

"Stop," Lily ordered. "Don't ignite the portal."

The group hopped off and ran toward Sunny. Lily and Michael held their swords against Ronan and Pablo's backs so they wouldn't escape.

Sunny was frantic. "Blossom fell in the lava river!"

"How?" cried Ilana.

"Are you sure?" asked Michael.

Lily remained calm. "Thankfully you both slept in Lisimi Village, so we know that she'll respawn there."

Sunny noticed a bunch of command blocks near a lava waterfall and, pointing at them, he screamed at Ronan and Pablo, "Did you put Blossom on Hardcore mode?"

"No," Pablo replied.

"We promise, we didn't," said Ronan.

"Then how did those command blocks get there?" Lily was angry. She knew someone wasn't telling truth. She was also scared that they could all be on Hardcore mode.

"Maybe Mr. Anarchy did this. Maybe he's trying to get back at us," suggested Pablo.

Sunny grabbed his sword and destroyed the blocks. "I don't care who left them here. Now they're gone."

Lily marched Ronan and Pablo back to the portal and called for Michael to ignite it, but he didn't. "Do you hear that?" he asked.

Everyone was silent.

"I don't hear anything." Lily was annoyed. "Just light the portal."

"I hear something," Michael protested.

This time everyone could hear a loud, high-pitched shriek, which grew more powerful by the second. They also heard someone cry for help.

"That sounds like Mr. Anarchy," exclaimed Peter.

"We need to find him," Lily called out.

She hopped off the portal, instructing Ilana and Peter to watch Ronan and Pablo. "Don't let them escape."

"We won't," Peter promised.

The gang ran toward the sound of Mr. Anarchy's cries.

"Oh no!" Simon gasped, when he saw Mr. Anarchy trying to battle a horde of blazes and ghasts on his own.

"I need help!" he cried out.

The gang shot arrows at the flying, fiery beasts. They were able to destroy a few, but there were so many flying through the sky that the battle seemed almost impossible.

Sunny aimed his arrow at a ghast, destroying it. Lily used her fists to deflect the fireballs. Mr. Anarchy used his bow and arrow to shoot at the mobs.

"Do you think Pablo and Ronan summoned this crop of blazes and ghasts?" questioned Lily.

"I'm not sure how they could have done that when they were with us the entire time," said Michael.

"And what about those command blocks?" asked Simon.

"Do you think there's another griefer lurking about?" asked Lily.

"I hope not," Simon replied as he destroyed another ghast with its own fireball.

"We have to get to the bottom of this," said Sunny. "I want to get back home. And I want to go to the

Overworld and find Blossom. She must be terrified that she's in Lisimi Village on her own."

"I'm sure she's with Robin," Lily reassured Sunny as she destroyed another blaze.

The battle was intense, even though there were just a handful of blazes and ghasts left floating in the sky. The gang annihilated the ghasts. Mr. Anarchy destroyed a blaze. "We're almost done with this battle," he called out as he destroyed another.

When the final blaze was destroyed, Lily asked Mr. Anarchy, "Where did you go? How did you disappear?"

He stood silently. He had no response.

Sunny questioned him, "Did you leave those command blocks by the lava waterfall?"

Again, he had no response.

"How can you expect us to trust you when you are keeping secrets?" Lily walked over to Mr. Anarchy and held her diamond sword against his chest.

"I don't want to lie to you," he told them.

"Then what are you hiding from us? Tell me!" Lily demanded as she clutched the sword, threatening to strike Mr. Anarchy.

"I didn't disappear," he confessed. "I saw someone the distance and I wanted to see who it was."

"Who was it?" Lily was angry.

A voice called out, "Remember us?"

Lily felt an arrow strike her back. She turned around and saw Emma, Otto, and Matthew aiming their bows and arrows at the group.

9
NETHER SURRENDER

"**E**mma!" Lily screamed. "Stop!"

Emma shot two arrows at Lily, piercing her skin making her lose hearts. Emma laughed. "Never!"

"How did you escape?" questioned Simon.

"You haven't been back to Lisimi Village in a long time. You have no idea what is going on there." Matthew smirked.

Lily's heart raced. What could be going on in Lisimi Village? Lily imagined the town under attack. She hoped Robin and Blossom were okay when they respawned. She hoped her small cottage was still standing. She hoped that Juan the Butcher still had his shop, and his friends Emily the Fisherwoman and Fred the Farmer were okay.

Lily screamed, "What did you do to Lisimi Village?"

"Surrender to us and you'll find out," ordered Otto.

"We're not going to surrender to you." Lily clutched her sword.

Michael leapt at Otto and struck him with his sword. Emma attacked Michael, splashing a potion of harming on him. Michael only had one heart left. Lily tried to give Michael a potion of healing, but it was too late. Emma struck him with her diamond sword and he was destroyed.

Emma smiled. "He's going to be in for a surprise when he respawns in the village."

"What did you do to the village?" Lily demanded. She struck Emma with her diamond sword.

While he skillfully battled them with his diamond sword, Simon shouted, "Tell us. You're monsters!"

Peter and Ilana ran toward the gang.

"Where are Ronan and Pablo?" Lily questioned while she battled Emma.

"I'm sorry." Peter held his diamond sword tightly. "They escaped."

Mr. Anarchy stood and watched the gang battle the trio of griefers. Simon looked over at him. "Aren't you going to help us?"

Otto shouted at Mr. Anarchy, "No, you work with us. You know how to play this game right. You know it's about survival and it's not about working together or building pointless theme parks that only distract you for a little while. You know it's all about control."

"I don't know," Mr. Anarchy stuttered. "I don't know what it's about."

"Help!" Lily cried as Emma slammed a diamond sword against her arm.

"I can't," Mr. Anarchy cried.

"You have to!" Lily was reaching out for Mr. Anarchy.

"How can you ask me to help you? You know why I can't," he pleaded.

"I'll give you milk. I'll make sure you won't get destroyed," she promised.

"I can't take that chance. Being on Hardcore mode means the end of me. I can't trust that Ronan and Pablo haven't put me on Hardcore mode," Mr. Anarchy said as he darted away from Emma's sword.

Lily intervened and struck Emma. Lily knew Mr. Anarchy possessed special skills that the other griefers seemed to lack. She had to get him off of Hardcore mode so she could convince him to use his intelligence to help others, but she wasn't sure how she could do it.

Mr. Anarchy was frozen. He didn't know what to do.

Otto aimed his arrow at Mr. Anarchy and struck his arm. Mr. Anarchy grabbed his arm. "Don't do that again, Otto."

"You're a traitor. You didn't help us escape, and now you're going to let us battle these players on our own. You aren't a griefer. You just cause grief!" Otto shouted.

Lily was shocked when the trio of griefers stopped battling them and started to attack Mr. Anarchy. He didn't fight back. He just grabbed some milk and drank it.

Simon cried out in pain when an arrow struck his arm. He turned around to see Pablo and Ronan sprinting toward him. He leapt at Pablo with his diamond sword, but Pablo just brushed off the blow.

"What's going on here?" Pablo questioned Otto and the others.

"Mr. Anarchy wouldn't help us fight," Emma replied as she pounded her sword into Mr. Anarchy's arm.

"Leave him alone," Pablo demanded. "He's useless."

"Useless," Mr. Anarchy repeated without any expression.

"We thought he knew how to get off this server, but he can't do anything. He doesn't even have our backs," said Pablo.

"When we needed you, you weren't there," added Ronan.

Mr. Anarchy didn't reply. He just looked at the group of griefers and, using his last bit of strength, he grabbed a potion of invisibility and splashed it on himself to disappear.

10

BACK TO THE OVERWORLD

"**W**here did he go?" Lily called out, but she didn't get a response. Instead Emma, Otto, and Matthew aimed their bows and arrows at her. When they fired, Lily was instantly destroyed.

Lily respawned in her bed and let out a sigh of relief. She was glad her house was still standing.

"Lily!" Robin called out. "You're here!"

"Where's Blossom?"

Robin spoke quickly. "She's been taken prisoner."

"By who?" asked Lily.

"I guess when we were gone, Otto, Emma, and Matthew escaped. They recruited the townspeople to be a part of their army."

"Recruited?" Lily was suspicious. She assumed Otto, Emma, and Matthew used fear tactics to convince all of the townspeople to become griefers. She hoped that she could reason with them.

"It doesn't matter how they got the entire town to join forces with them. The problem is that it's going to be a tougher battle than we ever imagined." Robin's voice shook. Lily knew Robin must have seen some truly awful things happen in the town to be this frightened.

Lily looked out the window, realizing that the sky was cloudy and it was raining. "Rain! Now we have to fight hostile mobs, too!"

"And we have to free Blossom," said Robin.

The duo didn't wait for the rain to stop. They sprinted into the center of town and made their way to the prison.

Lily felt an arrow pierce her back. "Ouch!" she cried.

"Skeletons!" Robin called out.

Lily turned around and saw an enormous skeleton army standing behind her. She grabbed a potion of strength and drank it, then grabbed another potion and splashed it on the skeletons.

"We have to destroy them while they're weak. I don't have that many resources left," Lily told her friend.

Robin and Lily struck the bony beasts, destroying multiple monsters. When each skeleton was destroyed, Lily picked up the bones they dropped on the ground.

"Watch out!" Robin called to Lily, but it was too late.
Kaboom!

The creeper exploded and Lily lost hearts. "I don't have any milk left," Lily cried as she spotted a horde of zombies lumbering toward them.

"We need help," Robin wailed as the rain fell and the hostile mobs continued to spawn in the dimly lit town.

Lily noticed a few familiar townspeople in the distance. "Maybe we can get them to help us."

"No!" Robin was frightened. "We have to get away from them. They attacked me before. They're also the same people who put Blossom in the bedrock prison. They believe we're the enemy."

"How can that be possible?" Lily thought this was a ridiculous idea, but she quickly changed her mind when the townspeople spotted them and started to shoot arrows at them.

"Surrender!" one of the townspeople called out.

"We're not your enemy," Lily pleaded.

Her inventory was low. She was cold. It was raining. There were zombies lurking close by, and she saw skeletons spawning in the distance. Lily was ready to surrender. She was fed up.

The townsperson shot an arrow at Lily. She only had one heart left. "You're our prisoner now."

Lily bowed her head, sighed, and surrendered.

Robin followed Lily as they were escorted into the bedrock prison that they had once constructed for Mr. Anarchy, Emma, Otto, and Matthew.

Though she didn't know what would happen next, Lily was happy to be reunited with Blossom.

"I can't believe they captured you," Blossom said.

"I know." Lily's head was down. She was devastated. "It appears that the entire town is now a part of a griefer army."

"Yes," Blossom explained, "Otto, Emma and Matthew convinced the entire town that we knew the way off the server. They said that we were the reason no one was getting back home."

"How could they believe that?" Lily questioned.

"Everyone is desperate. They'll believe anything." Robin tried to understand the reasoning behind the townspeople's decision to join the griefer army.

"How are we going to get out of here?" Lily moaned.

Lily was utterly surprised when she heard a voice call out, "I can help you."

11
COMMAND BLOCKS

"**M**r. Anarchy!" Lily couldn't believe it. "How did you find us?"

Robin quickly added, "And can you help us?"

Blossom questioned her friends, "Help us? But he's evil. He's one of them."

Lily's heart skipped a beat. She was waiting for Mr. Anarchy to realize his power and join them in their dream of escaping the server. She hoped he'd make the right choice. She looked at him and smiled. "Show them you've changed, Mr. Anarchy. Robin and I can't be the only ones who have noticed it."

"I want to change. I really do," he confessed.

"Why are you so evil?" Blossom questioned.

"Tell them, they'll understand," Lily said gently.

"But how can I? After all I've done?" he questioned.

"You're not the only one who lost hope along the way. We all have at some point, but you were zapped onto the server alone. We, at least, were together when we got stuck here. If I didn't have Simon and Michael, I might be bitter, too," Lily sympathized.

"How did you know I felt that way?" Mr. Anarchy smiled, and let out a sigh of relief. "You really understand."

"You don't have to be alone," Lily said. "Help us."

"How?" he asked.

"You've done it before." There was a twinkle in Lily's eye as she spoke to Mr. Anarchy.

"I will help you. I'm sorry I've caused all of this," Mr. Anarchy confessed.

"How can we trust you?" Blossom wasn't convinced Mr. Anarchy was telling the truth. "Weren't you zapping people onto this server just a few days ago?"

Mr. Anarchy had no response.

"What made you change your mind?" Blossom protested. "You just zapped Sunny and me onto the server, and now you claim that you're good. It doesn't make any sense."

Mr. Anarchy explained, "I thought Pablo and Ronan could help me with a plan I had for getting off the server. They questioned my power, and I had to find a way to prove it to them, which is why I zapped you and Sunny onto the server. I apologize for that, and I will do anything in my power to help both of you escape from this world."

"How?" Blossom wanted to go home very badly. Every time she thought about her home, she started to tear up.

"I have a plan that could get us off this server," said Mr. Anarchy.

"What is it?" asked Lily.

"It's rather complicated, and I need command blocks. All of my command blocks are in a stronghold in the jungle biome."

"How are we going to get to the jungle biome?" asked Robin.

"I'm not sure," Mr. Anarchy answered honestly, "but we're going to have to come up with a plan together."

"Where is everyone else?" asked Lily. "Where's Michael? He was destroyed and I thought he'd respawn in Lisimi Village."

"I saw Michael," Robin said. "He was battling townspeople. I tried to help him, but he disappeared. I'm not sure if he saw me."

"We have to find him, and the others," said Lily.

"Don't you think everyone will eventually end up here?" Blossom questioned.

"Yes, I'm sure they'll be captured. There's no doubt about that, since we are seriously outnumbered, but we can't wait around for them to arrive." Lily wanted to break out of the prison. She wanted to find her friends and she wanted to stop the townspeople. They had to realize they had made the wrong decision. She had to convince the townspeople that they had been tricked.

Mr. Anarchy said, "I know a way to escape. Does anybody have a pickaxe?"

Suddenly Lily remembered the hole on the floor that she had seen inside Mr. Anarchy's prison cell. She replied, "I don't have a pickaxe."

"I do," Blossom grabbed a pickaxe from her inventory.

"Could it be that we only have one pickaxe?" Mr. Anarchy searched through his inventory, but his pickaxe was missing. Robin couldn't find one either. "I guess we'll have to make do with this one." Mr. Anarchy banged his pickaxe into the prison floor.

Lily looked down and spotted a large tunnel. "Wow, can we really escape from here?"

"We have to keep digging the tunnel. I was never able to finish it," said Mr. Anarchy.

"How did you do this? This is a bedrock prison," Robin marveled.

Mr. Anarchy smiled. "A good magician never reveals the secret to his tricks."

Lily knew Mr. Anarchy still carried many secrets, and he was once one of the most powerful griefers in the Overworld, but she had to trust him as they climbed into the tunnel and made their escape from the bedrock prison.

12
SWAMPLAND

"Should we place a torch on the wall?" Blossom asked. "I've only been in a tunnel while playing the game, never while actually in it. Sunny and I were traveling to a stronghold and we placed a torch on the wall." Blossom began to sniffle as she reminisced about playing the game with Sunny.

Lily was stunned when Mr. Anarchy attempted to comfort Blossom. "It's okay. We will get you out of here. Don't cry."

Lily remarked, "Wow, you've changed, Mr. Anarchy." After checking her inventory, she added, "My inventory is empty. I don't have a torch. The only thing I have left is a diamond sword."

Robin had a torch, so she placed it on the wall. But the light wasn't strong enough to stop hostile mobs from spawning.

"Skeletons!" Lily shouted.

Three bony beasts aimed their bows and arrows at the gang. Mr. Anarchy ran toward the skeletons and struck one with his diamond sword.

Lily, Robin, and Blossom followed Mr. Anarchy, and together they slayed the skeletons. Mr. Anarchy called out, "It looks like it's all clear."

"How are we going to dig the rest of the hole? We only have one pickaxe," Lily reminded Mr. Anarchy.

"We're going to work together," he replied as he banged the pickaxe against the wall.

Lily was speechless.

Mr. Anarchy called out, "I see light!"

Blossom stood next to him. "Yes, I think we can crawl out of the hole."

Mr. Anarchy helped Blossom make her way through the small hole and onto a grassy patch. Lily, Robin, and Mr. Anarchy followed Blossom.

"It's getting dark," Mr. Anarchy commented as he looked up at the sky.

"Do you think we should build a house for the night?" suggested Lily.

"No, we're too close to town. It will leave us extremely vulnerable to the townspeople. They will be looking for us when they notice we've escaped," Mr. Anarchy said. Beckoning to them, he sprinted toward the next biome.

Lily bit her lip, but she followed the gang when everyone else ran after Mr. Anarchy.

After they'd run for a while, Mr. Anarchy looked up at the sky. "We have to build a house now. Soon it will be too late."

"Here?" questioned Lily. "On the edge of the swamp biome?"

"It's fine," Blossom said. "If we build it quickly we won't get attacked by slimes or witches."

Lily shuddered. "I guess we have to build the house super fast."

Everyone grabbed resources from their inventories and constructed the house. Lily didn't have anything in her inventory, and she felt useless. "What can I do to help?"

Robin handed Lily a wooden plank, and Lily helped construct the house with Robin's resources. As she placed the wooden plank on the ground, another bat flew close to her head.

"A witch!" Robin cried.

Lily turned to see a purple-robed witch rushing toward them. Lily grabbed the only thing left in her inventory, a diamond sword, and took a deep breath.

The witch leapt at Robin, splashing a potion of harming on her. Lily struck the witch with her diamond sword. The witch lost a heart but was able to splash a potion on Lily. Lily was weak and didn't have the energy to strike the witch again.

Mr. Anarchy sprinted toward the witch and fearlessly slayed the evil mob. The witch dropped a spider eye, and Mr. Anarchy picked it up and ran over to Lily.

He handed her milk and the spider eye. "Here, take this. I want to help you replenish your inventory. It's my fault that it's empty. I was the one who made you use up all of your supplies in unnecessary battles."

Lily sipped the milk and handed it back to Mr. Anarchy. He gave the milk to Robin, who drank it and restored her energy.

Robin thanked Mr. Anarchy. "I can't believe you're the same person who caused so much destruction in our lives."

"I'm sorry," Mr. Anarchy said and then hurried back to the house they were building. They had to finish the house before nightfall.

As they put the finishing touches on the house, Blossom heard a noise, and she paused. "What's that?" Blossom questioned.

Boing! Boing! Boing!

"It sounds like slimes!" exclaimed Lily.

Mr. Anarchy placed the door on the house. "The house is complete."

"Let's battle these slimes! We won't be able to sleep unless we do," Robin told the group. She sprinted in the direction of the slimes and slammed her sword into the first slime that approached them.

With multiple strikes from their diamond swords, the group was able to defeat the slimes. They were ready to go back to the house, when they heard a voice call out to them.

Lily couldn't see who was calling to them. She feared it was a townsperson who wanted to attack them.

She was exhausted from battling the swamp mobs and didn't want to engage in another battle, but she had to find out who was in the swamp.

Robin said, "I recognize that voice."

Lily heard the voice call out again.

"Help!"

"It sounds like they need our help!" Blossom walked in the direction of the voice.

Under a full moon, the group trekked through the dark swamp. They spotted Michael by the edge of a murky river, surrounded by slimes.

"Michael," Lily called to her friend, "we can help you."

Michael was losing hearts and he needed all the help he could get. Lily and the others annihilated the slimes. Mr. Anarchy handed Michael a potion of healing.

"Mr. Anarchy?" Michael questioned. "Why are you helping me?'"

"We'll explain later," Lily told him. "It's too dangerous to be out in the swamp biome at night. We just built a house. We can take you there."

The group ran toward the house. When they entered, they quickly crafted beds.

As Lily climbed into bed and pulled the wool covers over herself, she hoped she could really trust Mr. Anarchy. She wondered if he had truly changed his ways, or if this was a part of a larger, more sinister plan.

13
JOURNEY TO THE JUNGLE

When they awoke, Lily looked over at Mr. Anarchy's bed, but it was empty. "Where did he go?"

Robin woke up and looked at Michael's bed. "Michael is missing, too!"

Blossom walked toward the small window and looked out. "And it's raining!"

Lily paced in the small house. "I hope Mr. Anarchy didn't do anything bad to Michael."

The door rattled. Robin hollered, "A zombie is trying to break in!"

Blossom opened the door and splashed a potion on the vacant-eyed mob, then struck the undead beast with her diamond sword, destroying him. As she picked up the rotten flesh the zombie had dropped, she screamed, "There are tons of zombies out there. And two witches!"

Lily gasped. "Two witches! And all I have is a diamond sword!"

Robin handed Lily a bottle of potion. "This will help you if you get hurt."

Lily thanked Robin, and the trio ran out of the small house and straight into a soggy battle in the swamp.

Blossom destroyed a zombie, and Lily sprinted toward the witches. She knew that the more witches she destroyed, the more confident she would be when she encountered them in the future. With the potion in her inventory, she felt more certain that she'd survive the battle with the two witches.

The purple-robed witches darted toward Lily. She struck them with her diamond sword. One of the witches splashed a potion on her, and she didn't have the strength to strike them or retrieve the potion from her inventory. She was cornered. Her heart raced. Lily knew this was the end.

Just then, two arrows shot through the sky and struck the witches. Lily looked over and saw Michael and Mr. Anarchy sprinting toward her. The potion that the witch had splashed on her was losing its potency, and Lily was able to grab Robin's potion from her inventory and replenish her energy. Michael and Mr. Anarchy had bought her the time she needed to survive.

Lily joined Michael and Mr. Anarchy in a battle against the witches, and in a moment they had destroyed both mobs.

"Redstone!" Michael exclaimed when the witches dropped the valuable blocks.

"Let Lily have the redstone. Her inventory is very low." Mr. Anarchy handed the redstone to Lily.

"Thank you," she said as she placed the redstone in her inventory and then ran to Robin and Blossom to help them battle the zombies. Mr. Anarchy and Michael followed Lily.

As Lily slayed a zombie, the sun came out.

"The sun is out," Mr. Anarchy remarked. "We should travel to the jungle. We have to get the command blocks so I can get us off this server."

"Really?" Michael questioned. "You know how?"

The group walked through the swamp biome and into a lush jungle as Mr. Anarchy explained, "I have command blocks hidden in a stronghold. I was working with Pablo and Ronan on escaping from this server."

"How can you do that?" Robin asked.

"I have figured out how to create this intense lightning storm with the command blocks, and I know it will be powerful enough to zap a bunch of people back to the real world. It's very similar to the one that sent the Prismarines home." Mr. Anarchy described how he'd use the command blocks to summon this powerful storm.

"When can you do it?" asked Blossom.

"The minute we find the stronghold, I'm going to unleash the storm. We can all return home, and we'll never have to see this server again. It will be so nice to have a home-cooked dinner and to sleep in our own comfy beds."

"But what about Simon?" Lily couldn't get zapped back to the real world and leave one of her best friends behind.

"And Sunny?" Blossom added. "I can't go back to the real world without him."

"It's now or never. If we don't use the command blocks when we find them, we might never have this opportunity again," Mr. Anarchy said as he searched for the stronghold.

"I can't," Lily declared. "There's no way I will leave Simon."

"Me neither," said Michael.

"You have to think about yourselves. Don't you want to go home?" Mr. Anarchy asked as he sheared leaves and cleared a path through the lush jungle.

"I thought you had changed, but you really haven't changed at all," Lily said. "If you knew what it was like to truly care about people, you'd never ask us to leave our friends behind and only think about ourselves."

Mr. Anarchy wasn't listening to Lily. "Here it is! Follow me!" he said excitedly.

Lily stopped at the entrance to the stronghold and looked at the others. She was stunned to see them shrug and follow Mr. Anarchy inside.

14
CHOICES

"**M**ichael!" Lily called out.

"What?" He sounded annoyed. "We can't leave Mr. Anarchy alone. I promise I won't let him zap me back to the real world without Simon."

"What if he unleashes the storm and we have no choice?" Lily was worried.

Michael whispered, "We don't know if the command blocks are still in the stronghold. Maybe we are being tricked."

Lily hesitated, but after a moment she agreed with Michael, and they quietly walked behind Mr. Anarchy, Robin, and Blossom into the stronghold.

"There's a silverfish," Robin said, and she slammed her sword into the pesky insect.

"There's a lot more than one. It looks like a silverfish invasion," Lily cried. The ground was covered in silverfish.

"There must be a spawner nearby," Mr. Anarchy said calmly. "We have to find it."

"Do you think Pablo and Ronan booby-trapped this stronghold? If the command blocks were so valuable, they wouldn't just leave them here," Michael said as he slammed his sword into a horde of silverfish.

"That's a good point," Mr. Anarchy said as he walked deeper into the dimly lit stronghold, searching for the silverfish spawner.

Blossom looked off in the distance. "I see stairs. Are the command blocks upstairs?"

"No, they're here. But feel free to explore the stronghold. I have to look for this spawner. I can't summon the storm if we are in the middle of a silverfish invasion."

Lily questioned Mr. Anarchy's motivation for trying to deactivate the silverfish spawner, and she decided to follow him. "I'll help you find the spawner."

"Thank you." Mr. Anarchy smiled.

Blossom and Robin were tired of destroying silverfish. Blossom suggested they head upstairs to explore the stronghold.

Michael said, "Yes, you should go upstairs and escape the silverfish. It's pointless to destroy them when more will just respawn. I'll stay down here and help Lily and Mr. Anarchy."

Searching for the spawner, Lily, Mr. Anarchy, and Michael walked down a long, dark hallway. Nobody had a torch in their inventory, making them vulnerable to hostile mobs that spawned in low-lit strongholds.

"Watch out!" Lily called to Mr. Anarchy.

Three skeletons spawned and shot arrows at the gang. Mr. Anarchy leapt at a skeleton and destroyed it. Lily and Michael obliterated the remaining two skeletons.

Mr. Anarchy called out, "I found the silverfish spawner."

"But we don't have any torches. How are we going to deactivate it?" Michael wondered.

Mr. Anarchy said, "I'll just break it with my hands."

"Be careful," Lily warned him.

"I will." Mr. Anarchy crushed the spawner with his hands, deactivating it.

"Guys," Blossom called down to the trio, "we found treasure chests."

The group rushed upstairs and saw Blossom and Robin standing beside several unopened treasure chests. Robin asked Mr. Anarchy, "Why didn't you guys open these the last time you were here?"

"They weren't here," Mr. Anarchy replied.

"Maybe this is a trap," suggested Michael.

"But it's a treasure chest. I really want to open it," Blossom looked at the treasure chests.

"I don't think it's a trick," Mr. Anarchy said. "Treasure chests normally spawn in strongholds."

"Let's open it," Robin said, and she leaned over and took a deep breath before cracking open the first chest.

"What's in it?" asked Lily.

"Enchantment books!" Robin handed them out to the group.

Blossom opened the next chest and exclaimed, "Diamonds!"

Lily opened the next treasure chest. "Gold ingots!"

Michael and Mr. Anarchy opened the remaining chests, which were all filled with diamonds.

"Wow!" Lily was excited. "My inventory is brimming with all of these treasures. When I go back to Lisimi Village, I'm going to buy meat from Juan's butcher shop and have a large feast for all of my friends. And I'm going to go to the blacksmith and trade a lot of these treasures for a new pickaxe and other supplies."

"We aren't going back to Lisimi Village," Mr. Anarchy reminded Lily. "We're going downstairs, where I will summon a super powerful storm with my command blocks and send us all home. While finding these treasures has been exciting, they are pointless to us. We aren't going to take them back to the real world, because we don't want to have anything from this server. Once we get back to the real world, we get to start over. We will all join a new server and hang out with our friends. We can go back to school and be normal kids again."

Lily looked at her inventory and she thought about Lisimi Village. She realized that Mr. Anarchy was right. If she did leave the server, she'd never see Lisimi Village again. She'd never be able to ride on the roller coaster again. She'd never visit Juan's butcher shop or talk to Emily the Fisherwoman or Fred the Farmer. She hadn't realized just how much she'd miss this server.

"Let's go downstairs. I want to summon the storm," Mr. Anarchy told them.

"I can't go without Simon," Lily protested.

"Or Sunny," added Blossom.

A loud voice boomed across the musty stronghold, "You're not going anywhere!"

15

FINDERS KEEPERS

Pablo and Ronan stood by the stairs, their arrows aimed at the gang. Pablo shouted, "I see you found treasure. You can keep it."

"We don't need your permission," said Mr. Anarchy.

Ronan hollered, "Mr. Anarchy, you're coming with us. You have to summon that storm now. We have Matthew, Otto, and Emma waiting. We want to go back to the real world."

"Never!" Mr. Anarchy shouted. "I'll never help you leave this server. I want to know that you're trapped on here forever."

Lily screamed, "What did you guys do with Simon?"

Michael added, "And Peter and Ilana?"

"And Sunny?" Blossom wanted to see her friend again.

"They're all destroyed," Pablo replied with a sinister laugh. "We put them on Hardcore mode and destroyed them."

Ronan snickered, "We removed them from existence."

"What?" Lily was shaking. She hoped they were tricking her. "How could you do that to them? You are the worst people in the world."

"Yes, we are," Ronan said proudly.

"But they were our friends!" Blossom's eyes welled with tears.

Michael leapt at Ronan, striking him with his diamond sword. Lily shot Ronan with an arrow. Mr. Anarchy clutched his diamond sword and slammed it into Pablo. As a team, the gang destroyed the two griefers.

"Where will they respawn?" Lily asked.

"I don't know," Mr. Anarchy replied, "but we have to get Otto, Emma, and Matthew away from those command blocks. Those are our only way home."

Lily's heart pounded. She couldn't go home without Simon. She imagined sitting in Mrs. Sanders's classroom and seeing that Simon's seat was empty. She started to cry. She didn't want to go home. She wanted to find a way to see Simon again.

"Lily?" Michael asked, "Are you coming with us?"

Lily stared at Michael, who was waiting for her by the stairs. "I'm not sure. I don't think I want to be there when Mr. Anarchy's storm is unleashed. I can't go back to the real world without Simon. It would just be too painful."

"I know what you mean. But we also have to think about everyone else on this server. If we don't protect the command blocks, nobody will be able to leave."

"Why do I care about the other people on this server? They turned against us. They believe we're the griefers. They put me in prison. Let them get stuck on this server."

"Lily!" Michael was shocked. "This doesn't sound like you at all."

"Don't you care about Simon?"

"Yes, but we can't do anything about it. He was destroyed by evil griefers. What can we do?"

Lily didn't know what they should do. She just stood silently, feeling overwhelmed. The only thing she knew was that she missed Simon. "I don't know."

"Just come downstairs," Michael said softly. "We will figure this out together."

Lily followed Michael down the stairs. Mr. Anarchy was in the middle of an intense battle with Otto, Blossom was battling Emma, and Robin was splashing a potion on Matthew.

"Help!" Robin called out.

Lily struck Matthew with her diamond sword and asked, "Why did you have to destroy Simon?"

"Simon?" Matthew looked confused. "Destroyed?"

"Yes." Lily used all of her strength as she pounded her sword against Matthew's unarmored chest.

"Stop!" Matthew pleaded. "What are you talking about?"

"Pablo and Ronan said they destroyed him. They put him on Hardcore mode—" Lily couldn't finish the sentence. She starting sobbing instead.

"Simon isn't destroyed," Matthew said. "He's in the prison with Peter, Sunny, and Ilana."

Blossom stopped battling Emma and hurried over when she heard Matthew mention Sunny. "Where's Sunny? They told me he was destroyed and erased from existence."

"He's in the prison in Lisimi Village," Matthew said. But just then, Michael ran over to them and destroyed Matthew with a final blow from his diamond sword.

Mr. Anarchy obliterated Otto and Emma and called out, "The command blocks are still intact. I have to summon the storm before the griefers return. Are you ready?" Lily replied, "I can't go. I have to go back to Lisimi Village."

"Lisimi Village?" Mr. Anarchy was confused. "But they'll just put you back in prison."

"Matthew said that Simon was in prison with the others," Lily replied, "and I can't leave him."

"Matthew could be tricking you," suggested Mr. Anarchy.

"That's a chance I'm willing to take," Lily said. She had made up her mind. Turning on her heel, she sprinted out of the stronghold and back to Lisimi Village. She didn't even look back to see if she was alone.

16

THE SHOWDOWN

"Lily," Michael called out. "Wait for me!"

"Me too!" Blossom yelled as she ran, with Robin at her side. "But you're going to lose your chance to escape from the server," Lily told them. "If you come with me, we might be stuck here forever."

"I can't leave Simon," Michael said.

"And I'd never forgive myself if Sunny were stuck here and I went back home," Blossom added.

"I want to save Peter and Ilana," Robin said. "In fact, I don't want to leave this server if I know others are stuck on here. It's just too painful to think about."

As they approached Lisimi Village, they saw their old friends, Warren and George. Lily didn't say anything because she wasn't sure if their friends had been convinced that they were evil.

George spotted them. "Lily! Michael!"

"Please don't attack us," Lily pleaded.

"Why would I do that?" asked George. "Warren and I are working to stop this insane griefer army. We knew that Otto, Emma, and the others weren't telling the truth. We're trying to save Simon, Sunny, Peter, and Ilana."

Warren said, "They're trapped in the prison. We have to free them."

"Our plan is to free them, too." Lily was happy that they had additional help. She was hoping to free their friends before Mr. Anarchy unleashed his powerful storm and was able to transport them back to the real world.

"Lily!" a voice called out. Lily turned out and was shocked to see Mr. Anarchy sprinting toward her.

"I couldn't summon the storm and leave on my own. I understand what you were talking about," Mr. Anarchy said. "When you care about people, you just can't leave them." He paused, taking a deep breath. "I'm going to help you guys. We're going to save Simon, Ilana, and Peter."

They were steps from the prison when Juan the Butcher hurried over to them. "Watch out," he warned the group. "Emma, Otto, and Matthew are in town. I just saw them by the prison."

"Thanks," Lily said and then stopped. "Does anyone have a potion of invisibility?" she asked.

"I do." Robin took the potion from her inventory. As she handed out to the others, they heard Ronan holler at them.

"This is the end," Ronan screamed.

"No, it isn't," Mr. Anarchy said. "I've hidden the command blocks, and I'm the only person who knows how to summon that storm. You can't threaten us."

"I don't care if we go home anymore. If we're stuck here, I'll be able to torture you for the rest of time. I think I might enjoy it." Ronan unleashed a sinister laugh.

Mr. Anarchy was infuriated. He leapt at Ronan and struck him with his sword. Robin splashed a potion of weakness on Ronan and Pablo, and then said to Mr. Anarchy, "Don't bother with them. We have more important things to do."

Robin splashed a potion of invisibility on the gang and they sprinted toward the prison to free their friends. When they approached the prison, they were shocked to find ten guards in front of the door.

"There are so many people," Lily whispered as they walked past the guards and entered the prison.

The gang ran until they reached Simon, Ilana, and Peter.

Simon was pacing in the small cell. "I'm so upset. I bet Lily and Michael think we're destroyed."

Ilana said, "I'm sure they went back to the real world without us."

"What?" Simon was distressed. "They'd never do that. My friends would never abandon me."

"Neither would Blossom. She'd never let me down," said Sunny.

Peter agreed with Ilana, "It's a hard choice. If they had the opportunity to leave and they thought you were destroyed, I believe they might actually go back to the real world."

"Not my friends," Simon defended Lily and Michael. "They're the best people in the world. We would do anything to help each other out."

"I hope you're right. I hope they're not at home in their real beds or in their actual dining rooms eating real food right now. I hope they're somewhere in Lisimi Village trying to save you," Ilana said.

"But I'm telling you that you're probably never going to see them again," added Peter.

"Stop saying things like that. I believe in my friends," demanded Simon.

"And Blossom would never go back to the real world without me," said Sunny.

Ilana and Peter were dumbfounded when they heard Lily call out, "Simon!"

Blossom cried, "Sunny!"

Simon hollered, "We're in here! Save us!"

"They're really here!" Ilana was surprised.

"I told you they would come for me!" Simon was elated.

"I knew Blossom would save me!" Sunny was thrilled.

Lily, Michael, Warren, George, Robin, Blossom, and Mr. Anarchy broke into the small prison cell. They began to reappear, and Ilana gasped as she saw Mr. Anarchy standing in front of her.

"Mr. Anarchy?" Ilana stood against the wall, afraid of being attacked.

"Mr. Anarchy is our friend now," Lily explained. "And he knows how to get us off this server. He is going to summon a super powerful storm, and we will all be home in no time."

"Really?" Ilana cried tears of joy.

"Yes, really." Lily smiled.

"We have to get out of here before the guards see us. They're vicious," Peter warned them. "We've been trapped in here for several days, and they haven't fed us. Our health bars are very low."

Mr. Anarchy handed everyone apples and milk. "Eat and drink," he said.

Robin took out her last bottle of potion. "This is all I have left," she said, staring at the bottle, "but I think it's enough to make us all invisible. We just have to get by the guards, and then we can head back to the jungle biome."

"The jungle biome?" asked Peter.

"Yes. That's where Mr. Anarchy has stored all of his command blocks. He will summon a storm to get us all out of here," said Robin.

The gang gulped Robin's potion of invisibility. But once they ran out of the prison, they realized it wasn't strong enough; the potion was already wearing off.

"I can see my hands," Ilana cried.

Lily wasn't looking at her hands. She was staring at Otto, Emma, Matthew, Ronan, and Pablo. They stood in front of them, aiming their bows and arrows at the group.

Pablo demanded, "Where do you think you're going?"

"We're going home," declared Mr. Anarchy, "and you're not!"

Lily leapt at Pablo, but was distracted when she heard a thunderous boom. Rain began to fall on the group, and skeletons spawned in the distance. A skeleton's arrow ripped through Lily's skin.

A lightning bolt flashed through the sky, striking Otto. He disappeared.

"Did you summon this storm?" Lily looked at Mr. Anarchy.

"No," Mr. Anarchy replied. "This has nothing to do with me."

Another lightning bolt sparkled in the sky, and it hit Emma. She vanished.

Lily cried out, "What's happening?"

The townspeople rushed over and watched as the two griefers were struck by lightning and sent back to the real world.

One of the townspeople called out, "They said you were the only ones who could leave!"

Lily yelled over the thunder and the rain, "Don't follow the griefers. We only want everyone to escape."

"Even him? Mr. Anarchy?" questioned one of the townspeople.

"I want to help us all get back home," said Mr. Anarchy.

Lily clarified, "We can trust him. He's proven himself to us."

Another bolt of lightning flashed across the sky, and Matthew was struck. But he didn't disappear.

"What happened?" Matthew looked down at his hands. "Why am I still here?"

The sun came out, and Ronan started to scream, "It didn't work."

"What didn't work?" questioned Mr. Anarchy.

"You failed us!" Pablo slammed his diamond sword against Mr. Anarchy.

Mr. Anarchy shielded himself. "What are you talking about?"

"We used the command blocks, but they didn't work. You lied to us," shouted Ronan.

The townspeople crowded around Pablo, Ronan, and Matthew. One of the townspeople called out, "You guys are going to prison. You convinced us that Lily, Simon, and Michael were the bad guys, when it was you all along."

"No, they are bad," Matthew screamed. "Their new best friend, Mr. Anarchy, knows how to get off this server and he won't help any of you. They were going to leave from a stronghold in the jungle and abandon all of you here."

"That's not true," Warren called out.

"Matthew, I am going to get everyone off this server," Mr. Anarchy said. He paused. "Even you."

A townsperson ran toward Matthew with a diamond sword. "It's time for prison."

"No!" Matthew cried. But he had no choice; he was outnumbered as the rest of the townspeople crowded around him.

As the trio of remaining griefers were marched to the bedrock prison, a townsperson called out to Lily, "We're sorry we believed you were bad."

"It's okay." She smiled. "We all make mistakes."

Lily walked over to Mr. Anarchy. "You must be on the right track. I wonder if more people would have been able to escape if you had been the one who spawned the storm."

Mr. Anarchy smiled. "I'm going to work until I figure out how to create the perfect storm that zaps us all back to the real world. And I promise, I will be the last to leave. When I do leave, I will destroy this server."

Everyone cheered. Lily smiled at Mr. Anarchy.

17
GOOD NEWS

With the griefers behind bars, Lily, Michael, Simon, and Mr. Anarchy hurried back to the stronghold. Mr. Anarchy wanted to see if any of the command blocks were left in the jungle.

"It's empty," Mr. Anarchy said, giving up on looking for the blocks. "The griefers must have used them to summon that storm."

"We just need to get more command blocks, and then you can start working on the storm," said Lily.

"Yes," Mr. Anarchy said. "I want to start working on that as soon as I can."

"You know what I'd like to start working on?" asked Michael.

"The amusement park?" asked Lily.

"Yes," said Simon. "We were so distracted by this battle that we never got to work on our amusement park."

Mr. Anarchy said, "I've never taken a ride on your roller coaster."

"You have to try it!" Lily told him. "Now that you're our friend and not our enemy, I think you're going to enjoy being in Lisimi Village."

"But I still want to go home," Mr. Anarchy clarified. "I don't want to be stuck on this server forever."

"We all want to go home. But while we're here, we should have fun." Simon smiled.

Lily reflected, "When I thought that we were going to be zapped back to the real world, I realized that I'm going to miss Lisimi Village and all of our friends when we do go home. Once we leave this server, we won't see Juan the Butcher, Fred the Farmer, or Emily the Fisherwoman anymore."

"We should go back to town and enjoy our time there, now that we don't have to worry about you attacking us," Simon said. "I know we'll get home eventually."

Mr. Anarchy smiled. "I'm sorry that I was so awful. You're right: if we work together, we will all get off this server, and there won't be any distractions. I've been stuck on this server for such a long time, and being alone here made me so angry. I forgot what it was like to have real friends. Back at home, I had lots of friends and really enjoyed playing with them. It was very lonely being on this server without them."

Lily understood what Mr. Anarchy was saying. "I know that being trapped here can change you. Today, I began to resent the townspeople for listening to the griefers, and I didn't want to help them get off the server. In fact, I wanted them to be stuck here."

"When we get back to town, we will all work together to build the best theme park that ever existed in Minecraft," said Simon.

"We will ask all of the townspeople for help," Michael said with a smile. "We can finally have them work on a project that isn't destructive."

"That sounds like the best idea." Lily was excited to have the entire town work together to craft a large theme park.

Mr. Anarchy added, "I can't wait to help you build it."

"But first, you have to go on the roller coaster. It's so much fun," Michael told him.

The gang was about to leave the stronghold when Mr. Anarchy asked them to pause. "I see something," he said.

"What?" asked Lily.

"I see some command blocks!" Mr. Anarchy exclaimed.

The gang rushed over to the corner, where Mr. Anarchy helped him unearth the command blocks.

"This is a start," Mr. Anarchy said with a grin. "They didn't use all of the blocks."

"I wonder who will be the first person to leave the server." Michael said.

Mr. Anarchy placed the command blocks in his inventory, and the gang made their way back to Lisimi Village. On the way, they discussed who would be the first person to go home.

18
THEME PARK

Lily, Michael, Simon, and Mr. Anarchy walked into the town.

"Welcome back!" Ilana said, walking over to them.

Juan the Butcher raced through town and was very excited to see the group. "Do you guys want to have a feast, since you saved the town?"

"A feast sounds like a fantastic idea," Lily said, smiling. "But we have big plans."

"What are your big plans?" Peter rushed over.

"We're going to build a large theme park," Michael announced.

"An amusement park? With tons of rides?" questioned Ilana.

"Yes," Lily replied, "but first we're going to take Mr. Anarchy on his first roller coaster ride."

Mr. Anarchy corrected them, "I did ride a roller coaster once with my folks and my little brother. It was really scary. My mom bought the photo of us on the ride, and she put it on our refrigerator. I always laugh when I see it, because I look so scared and I was making a funny face."

Everyone was shocked to hear Mr. Anarchy reveal anything about his life before being zapped on the server. But Lily was happy to hear it. She had always suspected that Mr. Anarchy was a good person, deep down.

"Let's go on the roller coaster," Lily said. "You've never been on our coaster. It's the best."

"Lily." Michael looked over at his friend. "It sounds like you're bragging."

Lily blushed and then asked in raised voice, "Who wants to ride the coaster?"

The townspeople gathered around. Everyone wanted a ride on the coaster.

Michael added, "Who wants to help us build a theme park?"

The townspeople all shouted, "Me! I do!" Everyone was excited to start building the new theme park.

"We will hold a large meeting and start discussing the plans for the park," announced Michael.

Everyone cheered.

Mr. Anarchy and Lily walked toward the roller coaster. Mr. Anarchy was excited to go on it. "I can't believe I'm finally getting to go on the roller coaster."

"I can't believe you're not trying to blow it up," Lily joked as they climbed in the car.

The first drop was always the strongest, and Lily screamed as they dipped down.

"This is so much fun!" Mr. Anarchy smiled.

"Yes, and it's not over!" Lily said as they made the second dip.

When they got off the roller coaster, Michael was organizing groups, and everyone was starting to work on various rides.

Ilana remarked, "The village is so nice, now that it's peaceful."

Mr. Anarchy said, "I will make sure that Matthew, Pablo, and Ronan don't escape from the prison. I want peace in Lisimi Village."

"We know you do." Lily smiled. "Now, what ride do you want to help build?"

"I'd love to work on the carousel," Mr. Anarchy replied.

"Me too!" Lily was excited to build a carousel with her new friend.

As everyone worked on the rides, the town grew more excited for the new theme park. Lily smiled as she watched the town work together. She looked over at Mr. Anarchy. She had faith that he would be able to figure out a way to get them all off the server—but until they made it back home, they were going to create one super awesome amusement park. Lily couldn't wait to go on all the rides. She also had to admit that, once she left Lisimi Village, she would miss it.

READ ON FOR AN EXCITING SNEAK PEEK AT THE NEXT BOOK IN

Winter Morgan's Unofficial Minetrapped

Adventure series

Available wherever books are sold in July 2016
from Sky Pony Press

LISIMI LAND

ily looked down from atop the Ferris wheel and stared at Lisimi Land. She sat next to Simon and remarked, "I can't believe we've actually finished Lisimi Land. It's amazing!"

"That's what happens when people work together. You're right. Lisimi Land is terrific. It's such a super awesome amusement park." Simon smiled.

Lisimi Land was bustling. All of the townspeople were spending the afternoon enjoying the many thrill rides that filled the park. There was a long line for the roller coaster and another for the fun house.

"I think I've been on every ride." Lily scanned the park from the Ferris wheel.

Simon looked out as the Ferris wheel went around. "I haven't been in the fun house yet. Would you like to go again?"

Lily thought about the fun house. She liked it, but there were parts of the fun house that bothered her. The fun house gives you a texture pack that makes everything slanted. She paused; she didn't want to disappoint Simon, but she really didn't want to go through the fun house again. "Would you mind if I don't go to the fun house with you?"

"Why?" Simon was shocked.

"It's not for me. I find it slightly scary," Lily confessed.

"Scary?" Simon questioned. "We're stuck on a Minecraft server where we have battled every hostile mob in the Overworld, Nether, and the End, and you're scared of the fun house. That's funny, Lily."

"It's not funny." Lily was angry. "I was being honest with you. I didn't enjoy it."

Simon felt badly. "I'm sorry, Lily. I didn't mean to upset you."

"It's okay," Lily said. "I just don't want to be made fun of for admitting I'm afraid."

Simon smiled. "Remember how witches used to terrify you? And now you're not bothered by them?"

"They still bother me, but I'm not paralyzed by fear anymore. I've destroyed enough witches to know that I'll be fine if one of them tries to attack me," explained Lily.

The Ferris wheel ride was over. Before they stepped off the ride, Simon suggested going for another ride on the Ferris wheel, but Lily didn't want to. "Where do you want to go next?" asked Simon.

"I think you're right. It's very silly of me to be afraid of the fun house. I'm going to try going through it again."

"You don't have to do that. We can go on something else," Simon suggested. "How about the waterslide? Or the new roller coaster? Or bumper cars?"

All of Simon's ideas sounded great, but Lily wanted to conquer her fears. She wanted to go through the fun house again. "I really want to go in the fun house. It's the only part of the park that you haven't been in and I think you'll like it."

As Simon and Lily walked toward the fun house, they spotted Mr. Anarchy rushing toward them. He looked upset.

"Mr. Anarchy," Lily asked, "are you okay?"

Mr. Anarchy caught his breath. "No, something awful has happened. I was experimenting on a way to get off the server and I was with Warren. I think I accidently zapped him off the server."

"That's great news!" Lily exclaimed. "How did you do it? Now we can all leave."

"I'm not certain I zapped him off. I could have accidentally erased him from existence. I'm not sure." Mr. Anarchy spoke fast as his eyes welled with tears.

"What are you talking about?" Lily asked. "You have to take a deep breath and speak slowly. I want you to explain everything that happened."

Before Mr. Anarchy had a chance to reply, Juan the Butcher approached them. "Something is very wrong. I just saw a group of six creepers in the center of the town."

"What? That sounds like someone has spawned them," Lily cried out. "That could only be the work of a griefer."

Mr. Anarchy didn't want to hear about the creeper invasion. He was too upset over Warren's disappearance. "We can destroy the creepers, but we have bigger problems."

"What could be more important that a creeper invasion?" Juan the Butcher questioned.

"Warren's disappearance is more important." Mr. Anarchy took a deep breath as he told Juan what happened to Warren. "We were using command blocks to summon lightning that might zap us back to the real world when Warren disappeared. There wasn't a lightning bolt or anything. He simply vanished."

"How?" Lily questioned.

"I don't know," replied Mr. Anarchy.

Juan paused. "Do you think the creeper invasion and Warren's disappearance might be related?"

The gang wondered if this could be the case. Lily replied, "If that's true, we might have to battle a griefer."

"Has anyone checked on Pablo, Ronan, and Matthew?" asked Simon.

"I stopped by the prison on my way here and the guards were out front. It looked like everything was fine," said Mr. Anarchy.

"We have to get to the bottom of Warren's disappearance," Simon said.

"And we have to stop the creepers!" Juan warned them, as he pointed out several creepers that silently floated through the gates of Lisimi Land.

Lily grabbed her bow and arrow from her inventory and shot an arrow at a creeper.

Kaboom!

Simon and Mr. Anarchy also aimed their bows at the creepers, destroying the fiery mob with their arrows.

Ilana ran over to them. "What's happening? Why are there so many creepers in Lisimi Land?"

"I don't know, but we're going to find out," Lily promised her friend.

Lily stood in the center of the amusement park and made an announcement. "I don't want to frighten anyone, but it appears that there are a ton of creepers in Lisimi Village and this amusement park, Lisimi Land. We have to be very careful."

The townspeople all talked at once. Everyone was worried that they were under attack. Michael asked, "Is it a griefer?"

"We don't know," Lily replied.

A familiar voice called out from the distance, "I think I can give you some answers."

Lily was stunned. "Georgia? How did you get back on this server?"

Check out the rest of the
Unofficial Minetrapped Adventure series
and read what happens to Simon, Lily, and Michael:

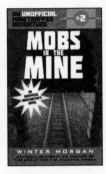

Trapped in the
Overworld
WINTER MORGAN

Mobs in the
Mine
WINTER MORGAN

Terror on a
Treasure Hunt
WINTER MORGAN

Ghastly Battle
WINTER MORGAN

Creeper Invasion
WINTER MORGAN

Attack of the
Ender Dragon
WINTER MORGAN

Available wherever books are sold!